*For my
lovely friends Ella Sky
and Isabelle Charlotte,
and Ella's
own Marius*

First U.S. edition 2015

Library of Congress Catalog Card Number pending
ISBN 978-0-7636-7476-2

14 15 16 17 18 19 CCP 10 9 8 7 6 5 4 3 2 1

Printed in Shenzhen, Guangdong, China

This book was typeset in Historical Fell Type Roman.
The illustrations were done in watercolor and ink.

Candlewick Press
99 Dover Street
Somerville, Massachusetts 02144

visit us at www.candlewick.com

LES MISÉRABLES

retold and illustrated by

Marcia Williams

based on the novel by

Victor Hugo

CANDLEWICK PRESS

POLICE NOTICE

It has come to my attention that you citizens known as "Les Misérables" believe that your wretched state of poverty and hunger is an excuse to flout the laws of France. You are mistaken. Every citizen must obey the law, and those who fail to do so will be punished.

Not a loaf of bread nor an apple from a tree will go missing without my learning of it. I will hunt down every criminal— rich or poor. The law shows no discrimination and no compassion.

I also warn all members of the revolutionary republican group "Les Amis de l'ABC" that your days are numbered. Should you seek to lead the miserable underdogs of our society to repeat the Revolution of 1789, you will fail!

The true citizens of France will not support you, and France will never again be a republic. King Louis XVIII is our monarch. He and the laws of France must be obeyed.

Inspector Javert, 1815

LONG LIVE THE REPUBLIC!

I wish I could read.

It might say how to find food.

Watch out— it's the cops!

BREAD OR DEATH

JEAN VALJEAN

It was October 1815 and Jean Valjean's first days of freedom. He had been imprisoned when he was just twenty-five years old for stealing a loaf of bread to feed his starving family. For this petty crime, Valjean had suffered nineteen years as a convict working on the galley ships at Toulon. He had not been a model prisoner and would long be remembered, by both convicts and captors alike, for his remarkable physical strength and his determined efforts to escape.

Yet now that he was a free man, Valjean felt no joy. He was without hope, and the cruelty of the last nineteen years had made his heart cold and bitter. As he tried to put as many miles as possible between himself and Toulon, the icy air off the Alps spread the chill to his very bones. He kept walking until evening, when he reached the city of Digne.

Valjean was a tired, hungry bundle of rags, and the locals of Digne shuddered as he passed.

After reporting to the mayor's office, as all ex-convicts had to do, Valjean went to an inn.

The innkeeper saw from Valjean's papers that he was an ex-convict and refused to serve him.

Valjean's reception was the same everywhere—at every house and inn. Even the guard at the prison sent him packing.

In desperation, he tried to escape the bitter air by crawling into a low hut, but he was met by the snarling jaws of an enormous dog.

Valjean was exhausted, and he collapsed onto a bench in the Cathedral Square. He lay there shivering until an old woman came out of the church. She gave Valjean her last four coins and urged him to make one more attempt to find shelter.

The modest house that the woman pointed to was occupied by the Bishop of Digne; his sister, Mademoiselle Baptistine; and their old servant, Madame Magloire. The bishop had never lived in the church palace but had given it to the townspeople for a hospital. He lived simply, and his door was always open to the poor, sick, and needy. Even tonight, when rumors of a dangerous stranger circulated around the town, the bishop would not lock his front door.

So, much to Valjean's amazement, he received a warm welcome.

"You didn't say *"Get out, dog!"*"

Slowly Valjean's hard, gloomy expression softened to one of delight.

"You have seen much suffering, but eat now."

"Your food is as simple as a wagoner's, but I'm grateful!"

Madame Magloire placed two silver candlesticks on the table. These, along with six sets of silver forks and spoons, were the bishop's only valuables. He had given the rest away to the poor.

"How do you know I'm not a murderer?"

"God will take care of that."

After dinner, the bishop handed a candlestick to Valjean and guided him to an alcove room, next to his own.

Valjean was exhausted. He did not even climb between the sheets but lay on top of the bed and fell into a sound sleep.

A few moments later, everyone in the little house was asleep.

As the cathedral clock struck two, Valjean awoke. He lay thinking of his years as a prisoner, of his poverty and his lost youth. He thought of many things, including the bishop's silver!

Valjean got up and crept into the bishop's room.

He saw that the bishop's goodness lit up his whole face.

For a moment, Valjean was overcome by emotion.

But the moment passed, and he took the silverware from the cupboard in the bishop's room.

He crept from the room, thrust the silverware into his bag, and jumped from the window.

He ran across the yard and disappeared into the night.

Unfortunately for Valjean, he was spotted by the local police and arrested. However, when they took Valjean to return the bishop's silver, they were all astounded: the bishop said he had *given* Valjean the silverware, as well as the silver candlesticks!

Valjean and the police all looked at the bishop in disbelief. When the police saw that he was serious, they left, and Valjean felt both bewilderment and gratitude. Why was the bishop being so kind to him, a thief?

The bishop fetched the candlesticks and handed them to Valjean along with the silverware. Then, before sending him on his way, he reminded Valjean that he had promised to use this wealth to become an honest man. A promise that Valjean could not remember making!

PETIT GERVAIS

At least you don't have to think in prison.

After leaving the bishop's house, Jean Valjean hurried out of Digne and into the open countryside. For the past nineteen years, Valjean had known nothing but hardship and cruelty and had long forgotten how to behave in an honorable way. He found the bishop's kindness disconcerting and was troubled by the idea of becoming honest. When evening fell!, Valjean lay behind a thicket to wrestle with his thoughts. He was disturbed by the sound of singing and saw a young boy sauntering toward him, tossing a coin into the air.

The coin fell to the ground, and Valjean, hardly knowing what he was doing, put his foot on it.

Petit Gervais pleaded for his coin, but Valjean, in a daze of hunger, did not seem to hear.

Petit Gervais tried shaking Valjean but still got no reaction.

Suddenly Valjean jumped up and grabbed his stick. Petit Gervais ran away.

A shudder ran through Valjean—his brow was hot with fever.

Slowly his mind registered the coin at his feet and the child he had stolen it from.

Valjean was overwhelmed with shame and ran after Petit Gervais, but the boy had vanished.

Valjean's legs buckled beneath him, and he fell to the ground. His heart swelled with regret and misery. He burst into tears.

FATHER MADELEINE

What is your name?

Father Madeleine.

Nobody knows how long Jean Valjean wept or where he went afterward. It is only known that sometime later a tall stranger entered the city of Montreuil and rescued the children of a police captain from their blazing home. The grateful citizens never asked to see this hero's papers but welcomed him to their city. Known as Father Madeleine, he soon brought hope and employment to the poor of Montreuil.

He established a successful glass-making factory and gave jobs to anyone who would work hard and was honest.

Father Madeleine invested his profits in hospitals and schools for the poor. His only display of wealth were two silver candlesticks.

The citizens loved him and after five years they appointed him mayor of Montreuil. There was just one man who failed to admire the new mayor . . .

Javert, the chief of police. Javert, who never forgot a crime or a criminal, was convinced that he had met the mayor before—and not as Father Madeleine!

One morning, Father Madeleine found Old Fauchelevent, an elderly man, trapped in the mud beneath his cart.

Inspector Javert was there, but neither he nor anyone else had tried to lift the heavy cart. They knew it would be impossible.

But Father Madeleine didn't hesitate. He removed his jacket and crawled under the groaning cart.

The great weight rose up onto Father Madeleine's back, and Old Fauchelevent was dragged to safety.

As Father Madeleine rose from the mud, Javert looked at him as though he were a ghost.

Old Fauchelevent was too badly injured to continue driving his cart, so Father Madeleine found him a job as the gardener at a convent in Paris. Old Fauchelevent loved the work, even though he had to wear bells on his knees to warn the nuns that a man was close by!

FANTINE

Father Madeleine's only interest in life was helping others, but his heart was never truly touched until he met Fantine. Fantine was a single mother struggling to care for her daughter, Cosette, on her own. When Cosette was nearly three years old, Fantine left her with the Thénardier family while she looked for work. The Thénardiers ran an inn near Paris and had two little girls of their own, Éponine and Azelma, so Fantine hoped that Cosette would become part of the family.

Fantine traveled to Montreuil and found work at Father Madeleine's factory.

A year went quickly by, but Fantine never seemed to have enough money to send for Cosette.

Then one day, the manager discovered Fantine had a child but was not married. He fired her.

Fantine despaired. How could she pay the Thénardiers without a job?

She tried sewing shirts but could not earn enough for Cosette and to feed herself.

The months went by. Fantine was close to starvation and developed a cough and fever.

Then Monsieur Thénardier wrote, asking for extra money for warm clothes.

Fantine sold her beautiful hair to a barber and sent Cosette a woolen skirt.

Monsieur Thénardier gave the warm skirt to his own daughter and wrote to Fantine again, demanding more money. Poor Fantine—in her mind Cosette remained the beautiful, happy child she had left behind, but the truth was very different. Little Cosette was treated as a slave by the Thénardiers and worked from dawn to dusk. She was dressed in rags and was fed under the table with the dog. Now, at the age of five, she was thin with misery and neglect.

Then Fantine received a letter from Monsieur Thénardier demanding forty francs. She felt completely helpless.

Yet that night she lay with a bloodied mouth and two gold coins. She had sold her two front teeth, believing she was saving Cosette.

Fantine had nothing more to sell, but Monsieur Thénardier's demands kept arriving.

As Fantine wandered the streets in misery, she became involved in a fight.

She was arrested by Inspector Javert and sentenced to six months in prison.

Then Father Madeleine stepped from the shadows and ordered Javert to release Fantine.

Fantine showed no gratitude but spat at Father Madeleine! In her mind, her every misery was due to his having fired her from his factory. He was horrified—he had known nothing about Fantine's dismissal. He insisted that Javert release her and promised to reunite her with Cosette and pay for their care. Javert was appalled that the law was being flouted, and Fantine could hardly believe her ears. She was so overcome by emotion that she fell into a faint.

Father Madeleine lifted Fantine from the ground and took her to the infirmary, where the Sisters of Charity could care for her. Then he sent some money to the Thénardiers and asked them to return Cosette.

JAVERT

Father Madeleine's money excited Monsieur Thénardier's greed. Instead of returning Cosette, he wrote asking for more money, so Father Madeleine decided to fetch Cosette himself. Unfortunately, his plans were upset by an unwelcome visit from Inspector Javert. Javert had come to inform the mayor that he had written to the Paris police to denounce him as the former convict Jean Valjean, suspected, since his release, of stealing a coin from a child.

However, the Paris police had replied that Valjean was already under arrest for stealing apples and was to be tried in Arras the following day.

Javert had come to admit his mistake and offer his resignation for this insult to the mayor. But Father Madeleine would not accept his resignation.

After Javert left, Father Madeleine spent the night fighting with his conscience. What was he to do? If he saved this man by disclosing his true identity, he would lose everything. Yet could he let another man be wrongly condemned to the galleys for life? It was not until the sun started its morning ascent that Father Madeleine finally set out for Arras.

Alas, I am in time.

Father Madeleine rode hard, stopping only once to repair his gig, and arrived in Arras that evening.

Shall I come to this again?

The man in the dock looked just like his former self—the bitter convict Jean Valjean!

Release that man. I am Valjean.

Father Madeleine told the jury that he, not the accused, was Jean Valjean.

Are you mad?

No.

There was a stunned hush, but no one moved to arrest Father Madeleine—a mayor!

Since I am not arrested and I have things to do, I'm going.

So Father Madeleine—or Jean Valjean, as we now know him to be—left the court, hoping he would have time to reunite Cosette and Fantine before he was arrested.

And Cosette?

Later. First you must get well.

When Valjean returned to Fantine's bedside, she hoped that the man she knew as Father Madeleine would have Cosette with him.

Good God! What is the matter, Fantine?

For a moment Fantine smiled—then she half rose from her bed and her eyes widened in terror!

Jean Valjean turned to see that Inspector Javert had entered the room!

He begged Javert for three more days of freedom to fetch Cosette.

But Javert refused. He was not letting go of his quarry a second time!

Fantine started in horror, then sank back onto her pillows—dead.

Valjean shrugged off Javert. He gently closed Fantine's eyes and kissed her hand.

Javert put Valjean in the city prison, but Valjean used his great strength to break a bar on the window and escape. He remained free for only three days before being recaptured and tried for robbing Petit Gervais. All the good he had done as Father Madeleine was forgotten. He was sentenced to the galleys for life.

PRISONER 9430

Hurrah, he deserves to be pardoned!

In October 1823, Jean Valjean, convict number 9430, was serving on the *Orion* when a sailor fell from the top rigging. He managed to grab hold of a rope, but it quickly began to slip through his hands. Nobody moved, except Valjean. He crawled up onto the rigging and used his great strength to haul the sailor back to safety. The onlookers cheered, but then let out a cry as Valjean slipped and fell into the sea. Everyone waited, but he didn't rise to the surface. It was reported that convict number 9430 had drowned.

COSETTE

It was Christmas night. For some, this meant gaiety and gifts. For Cosette, now eight years old, it meant that the Thénardiers' tavern was busier, she had to work harder, and Madame Thénardier beat her more frequently. So Cosette did not dawdle as she went to fetch water from the well, though the path down the wooded hill was full of strange noises and shadows.

Even empty, the bucket was heavy, and as Cosette's frozen hands clutched the full bucket, she felt her strength leave her. Then out of the darkness a huge hand reached down and took the bucket from her. Cosette looked up into the eyes of a tall, smiling stranger. Cosette did not know it, but he was Jean Valjean.

Back at the inn, Valjean offered Thénardier a large sum of money to release Cosette into his care.

After much bargaining, Valjean and Cosette set off for Paris, but not before Cosette was dressed in warm clothes and given a new doll.

During Valjean's brief escape from the city prison, he had hidden his money and the candlesticks, so he was rich. However, he still feared that Javert would discover him, so he and Cosette took modest lodgings in a poor area of Paris.

Yet to Cosette, her new home was luxury. She could hardly believe she did not have to work!

As the weeks went by, Cosette learned to laugh and play, and Valjean learned to love.

We'll have to move.

Then, one day, Valjean heard heavy footsteps. Javert had found him!

At dusk, Valjean and Cosette crept from their lodgings.

Javert was soon on their trail!

Valjean picked up Cosette and ran.

Suddenly they reached a dead end!

There was a high wall in front of them.

My brave Cosette.

Valjean cut a rope from a street lamp and tied it around Cosette.

Search the cul-de-sac!

He scaled the wall, then hauled Cosette up.

With Cosette in his arms, he jumped into the garden beyond.

My precious Cosette.

They had escaped Javert, but now Cosette was shivering and needed warmth and shelter.

Valjean decided he would have to ask the gardener for help and risk being handed over to Javert.

Did you fall from the sky?

Will you hide us?

Imagine Valjean's relief—the gardener was Old Fauchelevent, and this was the convent garden where he worked!

Now I can repay my debt to you.

Fauchelevent was delighted to help the man who had saved his life, and Cosette was soon sitting beside his warm fire.

Child, concentrate!

Valjean and Cosette stayed safely hidden in the convent grounds for the next five years. Valjean helped Fauchelevent in the garden while the sisters educated Cosette. She grew from a skinny young girl into a beautiful young woman.

MARIUS PONTMERCY

When Old Fauchelevent died, Valjean decided that he must finally be safe from Javert, and that he and Cosette could leave the sanctuary of the convent grounds. They moved to a small house in Paris, close to the Luxembourg Gardens, where they would walk each day. It so happened that Marius Pontmercy, a poor young man who had once studied law but now earned a meager living in a bookshop, was also in the habit of walking in the gardens. One glorious summer's day, as he wandered aimlessly along the paths, he passed Cosette, and his life was never quite the same again. He had fallen in love at first sight!

Day after day for nearly a year, Marius returned to the gardens, hoping to see Cosette.

His friend Enjolras tried to distract him, urging him to join the Friends of the ABC, a group of revolutionaries. Without a proper income, Marius had nothing to offer such a beautiful young girl. But he would not be distracted.

Then Marius's dream came true—Cosette met his glance and he saw that she returned his love! Now both Marius and Cosette lived for their walks in the gardens and the stolen glances that passed between them.

Marius became bolder and always remained close to Cosette in the gardens: behind a tree or a book, on a nearby bench or following her footsteps.

Valjean began to notice and worried that Javert was having him followed.

Then one day Marius made the mistake of following Cosette home, which aroused Valjean's suspicions even further.

Valjean decided to move quickly to another district without leaving an address. The months passed. Marius walked the streets of Paris searching for Cosette, but she seemed lost to him. His mood grew dark with despair.

Marius had rooms in a poor tenement. The only other people living there were the Thénardier family. Monsieur Thénardier had grown a beard, changed the family name to Jondrette, and moved to Paris to escape his many debts. Without the inn to run, he spent his time writing letters to benevolent rich people, begging for money. Marius hardly noticed his neighbors, but Éponine, the elder daughter, had noticed *him*, and she often tried to attract his attention. Poor Éponine—she soon realized that Marius's heart was engaged elsewhere!

Although Marius's thoughts were mostly with Cosette, he was curious about his neighbors, so one evening he climbed on his bureau to look through a crack in the wall. The filthy state of the garret horrified him. Monsieur Thénardier was seated at a table, writing. His wife was squatting on the floor, and their youngest daughter lay on a pallet. Just then the door opened and Éponine appeared. She had news: one of their benevolent patrons was about to arrive.

There was a rap on the door, and in walked Jean Valjean with Cosette. Marius nearly burst into tears of delight.

Cosette was carrying a large bundle of clothes, but all Thénardier wanted was money.

Valjean agreed to return later with some money, and in the meantime he gave Thénardier his coat.

When they left, Thénardier started talking excitedly—he had recognized Valjean from the inn, eight years before!

Thénardier formulated a wicked plan to trick Valjean out of a fortune and then murder him.

Marius rushed to the police station, where he told an inspector all he had overheard.

The inspector gave Marius two pistols to fire into the air if things turned nasty.

The police inspector was Jean Valjean's old enemy, Inspector Javert!

Marius returned home and waited at his spy hole until Valjean returned with the money.

Thénardier appeared grateful until his gang of thugs arrived—then he turned into a wild beast.

He told Valjean that he was the innkeeper Thénardier and that now he wanted proper payment for Cosette.

Marius was about to fire a shot to warn the police when Valjean made a dive for the window. But Valjean wasn't quite quick enough, and the bandits hauled him back.

Thénardier continued to abuse Valjean . . .

until Valjean broke his bonds and leaped at him.

Again Marius was about to fire his pistol, but this time the door flew open and Javert burst in. Valjean took advantage of the confusion and vanished out the window. Thénardier and his thugs were all arrested.

MARIUS AND COSETTE

Marius asked Éponine if she could find Cosette's address for him and promised to reward her well. Then he left his dingy lodgings next to the Thénardiers and moved in with Enjolras. Enjolras and the other Amis de l'ABC were busy gathering arms and recruits for a protest against the government and king. They wanted greater freedom of speech and justice for the poor. Marius, who could only think about finding Cosette, refused to join them.

For two months, Marius heard nothing from Éponine. While the revolution drew ever closer, he searched the streets of Paris for Cosette.

Then, in April, Éponine brought him Cosette's address.

She reminded Marius that he owed her a reward.

Marius gave her five francs. Éponine let the coin fall and looked at Marius with sadness.

That evening, Cosette found a packet of love poems hidden in her garden.

The next evening, Cosette found Marius waiting for her in the garden.

They talked all through that night and met secretly every evening in April and May.

Meanwhile Valjean was growing increasingly concerned that another revolution was brewing in Paris.

Valjean was determined to escape, and Cosette and Marius felt desperate.

Marius had no family, except a wealthy grandfather with whom he had quarreled. He decided to swallow his pride and ask his grandfather for the money to marry Cosette. He left Cosette full of hope.

The following evening, Marius returned to the garden to tell Cosette that his grandfather had refused him the money. But the house was deserted—Cosette had gone. Without Cosette, Marius's life seemed worthless. He finally decided to join Enjolras and Les Amis de l'ABC. He knew they were preparing for violence and already barricades were being erected in the streets. He would give his life to their cause!

THE BARRICADE

If you blow up the barricade, you'll blow yourselves up, too!

It was the day of General Lamarque's funeral. He had championed the city's poor, Les Misérables, and his funeral was a chance for their supporters to protest against the government. A group of protestors tried to take the general's coffin from the soldiers. Two shots were fired, and suddenly the fighting began. Enjolras and Les Amis de l'ABC had built a barricade in the market district of Paris, and when Marius got there, soldiers were already attacking it. The protestors were poorly armed, and some of them were no more than children.

Marius could see that his friends were about to be overwhelmed. He grabbed a torch and made his way to a powder keg. He did not notice a soldier take aim at him—nor did he notice a ragged boy jump in front of him as the soldier fired the bullet. There was a sudden silence as the soldiers paused to reload. Marius grabbed the powder keg and yelled to the soldiers to retreat or he would blow up the barricade. Not caring whether he lived or died, Marius lowered the torch toward the gunpowder. Within seconds, the soldiers had fled into the night.

As Marius's friends gathered around their hero, Marius heard a faint voice at his feet. Bending down, he found Éponine, dressed as a boy. She was the "ragged boy" who had protected him from the soldier's bullet. Now she was close to death but had one more gesture of love for Marius: in her pocket, she had a letter from Cosette, which she gave him in return for a kiss on her forehead. Éponine died with a smile on her lips, close to the one she loved.

To Monsieur Marius Pontmercy, rue de la Verrerie, No. 16
My beloved,
Alas, my father wishes to set out immediately.
Tonight we shall be at the rue de l'Homme Armé,
No. 7. In a week we shall be in England.
Cosette
June 4th

Marius laid Éponine gently down and went to find a candle to read his precious note.

His first thought was that he need not die: Cosette loved him!

Yet he still had no money, and she had gone away.

He tore a page out of his notebook and scribbled a message.

He gave it to Gavroche, a young messenger, to deliver to Cosette.

Give it to the lady. I'm off to fight at Chanvrerie.

Gavroche wanted to join the protest, so he ran all the way and then thrust the letter into the hands of Valjean, who read it:

Our marriage is impossible. I have asked my grandfather; he has refused. I am without a fortune, and so are you. I ran to your house but did not find you. I love you.
I go to fight and to die. When you read this, my soul will be near you, and I will smile upon you.
Marius

Cosette married . . . no!

It's good he'll die!

But she'd be so sad.

I'll have to save him!

Valjean was shocked to think that Cosette planned to leave him for Marius, but he realized that if Marius was killed, her heart would be broken, and that would be worse. He would have to rescue him.

Valjean arrived at the barricade during a pause in the fighting, but the citizens had already suffered many losses.

Inspector Javert, who had always detested Les Amis de l'ABC, had been caught spying—but not one bullet could be spared to shoot him.

Suddenly there was a cry from the barricade as the artillery blew a great hole in the defenses.

Valjean ran through a storm of bullets, grabbed a mattress, and stuffed it into the opening.

The attack was relentless, and the revolutionaries were losing badly. So when Valjean offered to shoot Javert, nobody objected.

Valjean took Javert down a dark alley, but instead of shooting him, he fired his pistol into the air and told him he was free to go.

As Valjean returned to the barricade, the drum beat another charge and again the soldiers were upon them. The attack was like a hurricane! Through the cloud of combat, Valjean saw that Marius had been wounded in the shoulder. As Marius lost consciousness, Valjean lifted him up and carried him away.

The army and the police were closing in on all sides, and there seemed nowhere to escape to. Then Valjean saw an iron grating level with the ground. He had no time to hesitate: he lifted the grating and jumped into the putrid darkness below.

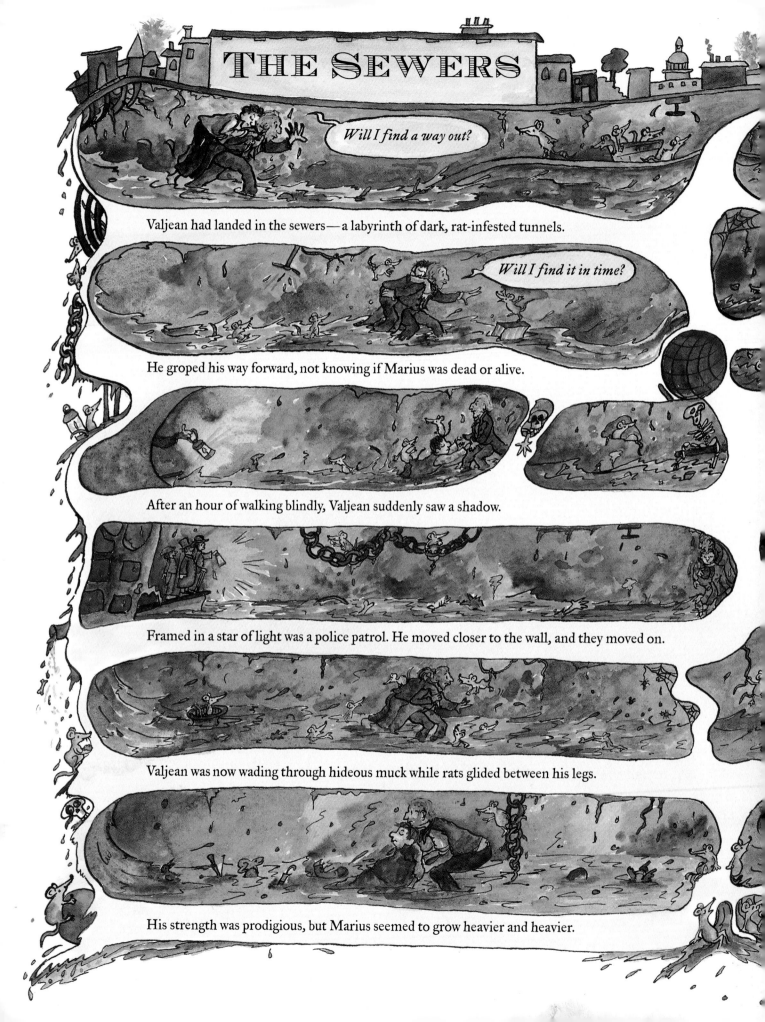

THE SEWERS

Will I find a way out?

Valjean had landed in the sewers—a labyrinth of dark, rat-infested tunnels.

Will I find it in time?

He groped his way forward, not knowing if Marius was dead or alive.

After an hour of walking blindly, Valjean suddenly saw a shadow.

Framed in a star of light was a police patrol. He moved closer to the wall, and they moved on.

Valjean was now wading through hideous muck while rats glided between his legs.

His strength was prodigious, but Marius seemed to grow heavier and heavier.

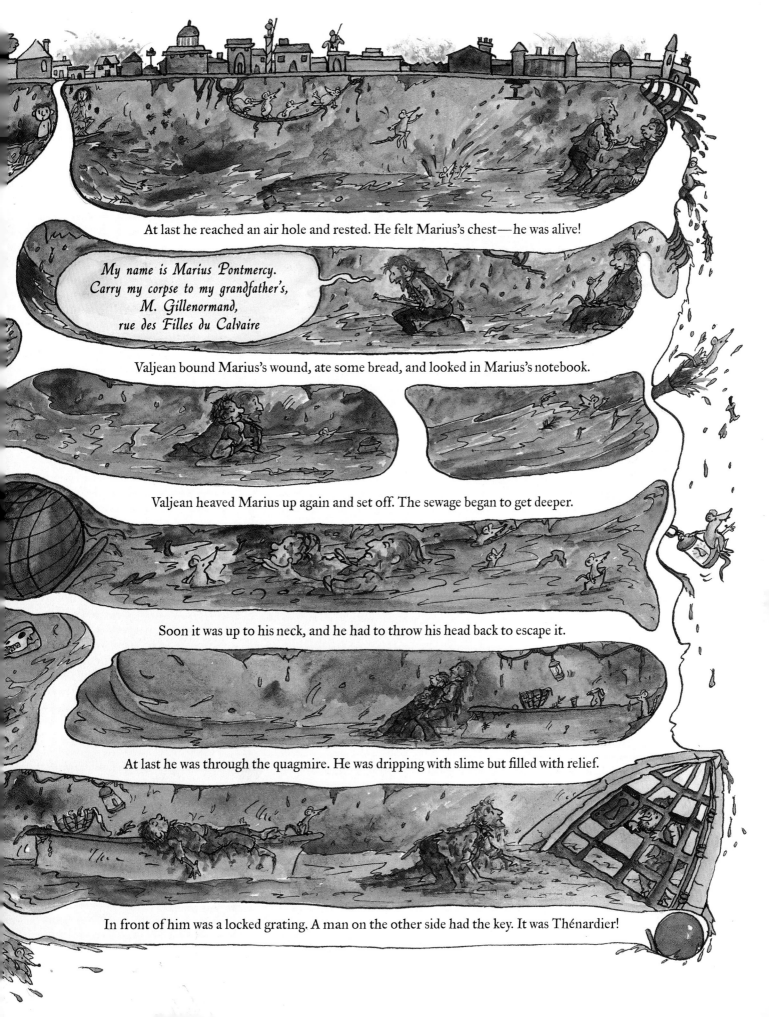

At last he reached an air hole and rested. He felt Marius's chest—he was alive!

My name is Marius Pontmercy.
Carry my corpse to my grandfather's,
M. Gillenormand,
rue des Filles du Calvaire

Valjean bound Marius's wound, ate some bread, and looked in Marius's notebook.

Valjean heaved Marius up again and set off. The sewage began to get deeper.

Soon it was up to his neck, and he had to throw his head back to escape it.

At last he was through the quagmire. He was dripping with slime but filled with relief.

In front of him was a locked grating. A man on the other side had the key. It was Thénardier!

Luckily Thénardier didn't recognize Valjean, and after Valjean had given him all the money he had on him, Thénardier unlocked the grating. Once outside, Valjean felt a strange uneasiness. He turned around, and there was Javert! Javert grabbed hold of him and held on like a lynx, but Valjean begged to return Marius to his grandfather before being imprisoned. Javert was amazed that Valjean should consider him capable of such a concession, but he did not refuse. Valjean laid Marius on the seat of Javert's carriage, and off they went.

Then I am yours.

I will wait here for you.

After Marius had been delivered to his grandfather's house, Valjean asked to be allowed home to see Cosette.

When they arrived at Valjean's address, both men got out. Valjean went inside, but Javert did not follow.

Must I spare his life as he spared mine?

When Valjean reached his bedroom, he looked out the window. Javert was gone!

Javert walked off toward the river Seine. He was overwhelmed by misery and confusion.

Javert had lived for the law, yet Valjean, whom he had treated like a worthless criminal, had spared his life and shown him kindness and compassion. He could not bring himself to arrest Valjean, nor could he let him go free. He felt his life no longer held any meaning. He climbed onto the parapet above the Seine, fell forward into the darkness, and disappeared under the water.

THE WEDDING

Marius's grandfather, Monsieur Gillenormand, had not welcomed his grandson when he asked for money to marry Cosette, but now that Marius lay injured, Monsieur Gillenormand cared for him with great love. Every day, Valjean came to inquire after Marius and deliver bandages made by Cosette. As Marius grew stronger, he began to mourn his friends who had been killed at the barricade and to wonder who had saved his life. His only other thought was of marrying Cosette, and this time his grandfather did not refuse his permission. In February, when Marius had recovered, the pair were married. Valjean gave Cosette his fortune as a wedding gift.

Early the following day, Valjean called on Marius and revealed his secret past as a convict.

Valjean asked Marius not to tell Cosette.

Marius was horrified by Valjean's confession and the disgrace an ex-convict might bring to his family.

Marius tried to drive Valjean away. He did everything in his power to make Valjean's visits to Cosette uncomfortable.

Valjean was deeply hurt. His visits to Cosette became fewer and fewer, until they stopped altogether.

Cosette felt heartbroken. She had thought of Valjean as her father and was at a loss to understand his rejection.

A few days after Valjean's last visit to Cosette, Thénardier called on Marius. He hoped to sell Marius a secret about Jean Valjean.

Thénardier recounted how, on the night of the barricades, he had found Valjean in the sewers with the body of a man he had murdered.

Suddenly everything became clear to Marius—*he* had been the "body." Valjean had saved his life!

Marius threw Thénardier out and ran to tell Cosette to make haste: they had to visit her father.

At his lodgings, Valjean lay haggard and wretched. His heart was broken by the loss of Cosette. When Marius and Cosette entered his room, he turned his head feebly. The only light came from the mantelpiece, where the bishop's two candlesticks stood, and in the gloom, Valjean doubted his eyes.

Cosette was overwhelmed by emotion. She and Marius wanted to take Valjean home with them, but Valjean knew that he was very close to death. Cosette and Marius fell on their knees beside him, stifling their tears. Valjean's hands rested on their heads and did not move again. He lay back with his head turned to the sky, and the light from the two silver candlesticks fell upon his face.

He sleeps. Although much to him was denied,
he lived, and when his dear love left him, died.
It happened of itself, in the calm way
that in the evening, nighttime follows day.